The Princess and the Wizard

About the author and illustrator:

Julia Donaldson has written some of the world's favourite picture books. She also writes books for older children, as well as plays and songs, and she spends a lot of time on stage performing her brilliant sing-along shows! Julia may not be a real princess but when she was little she pretended her cat, Geoffrey, was a prince, and she argued with her sister over who would marry him.

Lydia Monks is an award-winning illustrator with many picture books to her name. She has illustrated characters as varied as a ladybird, a rabbit, a mermaid and a spider. Lydia also loves to draw things for her two little girls, especially princesses, but definitely not wicked wizards.

For Eve ~ J.D.
For Princess Amelia ~ L.M.

First published 2006 by Macmillan Children's Books
This edition published 2013 by Macmillan Children's Books
an imprint of Pan Macmillan
20 New Wharf Road, London N1 9RR
Associated companies throughout the world
www.panmacmillan.com

ISBN: 978-1-4472-8214-3

Text copyright © Julia Donaldson 2006
Illustrations copyright © Lydia Monks 2006
Moral rights asserted

2 4 6 8 9 7 5 3

A CIP catalogue record for this book is available from the British Library.

Printed in China

The Princess and the Wizard

Julia Donaldson

Illustrated by Lydia Monks

MACMILLAN CHILDREN'S BOOKS

It was Princess Eliza's birthday. She was just blowing out the seven candles on her cake when a wicked wizard flew down the chimney and into the room.

"WHY DIDN'T YOU INVITE ME TO YOUR PARTY?" he thundered.

"Because wicked wizards like turning people to stone," replied Princess Eliza.
"So they do," said the Wizard, and with a flick of his bony fingers he turned the King, the Queen and all the party guests into stone. Then he laughed a horrible laugh and said to Princess Eliza, "They like capturing princesses too."

Just then there was a whirring of wings and in through the window flew the Princess's Fairy Godmother. She was late for the party.

When she saw what had happened, she waved her wand and said:
"The Princess may try seven times to escape
By changing her colour and changing her shape."

The Wizard just laughed his horrible laugh and said:
"Changing her colour and changing her shape
Will never help Princess Eliza escape."

Then he snapped his bony fingers again and
turned the Fairy Godmother to stone.

The Wizard whisked the Princess up the chimney
and carried her away to his tall dark castle.
He locked her into the cellar, where she cried
herself to sleep.

The next day was Monday. The Wizard unlocked the cellar door. He was holding the big red book which contained all his magic.

"This is your first chance to escape," he said. "I shall count to one hundred and then I shall come and find you."

He opened his book, closed his eyes and began to count.

Eliza ran outside. The moat of the castle
under the blue sky. She jumped into
d turned herself into a blue fish.

9

"Ninety-eight, ninety-nine, a hundred!"
The Wizard opened his eyes, looked in
his magic book and read:
To find where Eliza is hiding from you,
Look in the moat for the fish that is blue.

He fished Eliza out of the moat and
took her to his kitchen, which was full
of blue plates and pots and pans.
They were all covered in dried-up food.

"So you like blue, do you?" he said.
"Then set to work and wash!"
And he locked her in.

On Tuesday morning the Wizard unlocked the kitchen door. He looked at the clean plates and pots and pans and he grunted.

"Chance number two," he said. Then he opened his book, closed his eyes and began to count.

Princess Eliza ran to the farmyard.
She turned herself into a yellow chick
and hid in some straw.

But the Wizard read in his book:
The straw in the farmyard is yellow and thick.
Princess Eliza's disguised as a chick.

He scooped Eliza up and took her to a cupboard
which was full of yellow socks. They all had holes
in them, made by his pointy toenails.

"So you like yellow, do you?" he said.
"Then set to work and darn!"
And he locked her in.

On Wednesday morning the Wizard unlocked the cupboard door, looked at the darned socks and grunted.

"Chance number three," he said, and he opened his book, closed his eyes and began to count.

Princess Eliza ran to the meadow. She changed herself into a green grasshopper and hid among the grass blades.

But the Wizard read in his book:
The grasshopper princess is easily seen
Chirping away in the meadow so green.

He caught Eliza in a net and took her to his green bathroom. The bath, basin, walls and floor were covered in the Wizard's slimy toothpaste.

"So you like green, do you?" he said.
"Then set to work and wipe!"
And he locked her in.

Three more days went by. Each day the Princess tried to escape.

On Thursday she turned herself into an orange fox and hid in a pile of orange leaves.

On Friday she turned herself into a purple butterfly and fluttered among some purple flowers.

On Saturday she
turned herself into
a black cat and lurked
in a black tunnel.

But each time the Wizard
found her and gave her
yet more work to do.

On Sunday morning, the Wizard came on to the roof where Eliza had been scrubbing the sooty chimney pots. Instead of grunting, he laughed his horrible laugh.

"This is your last chance," he said. "If I catch you this time, you must stay and work for me for the rest of your life." Then he opened his book, closed his eyes and began to count.

Princess Eliza turned herself into a white gull and flew up into a cloud. But as she hovered above the roof where the Wizard was still counting, she saw words forming on the page of his open book. "So that's how he finds me!" she cried. "I shall never escape!"

Then she had an idea.
She turned herself
into a page of the
Wizard's book —

a perfectly blank
white page, with
no writing on it.

23

"Ninety-eight, ninety-nine, a hundred!"
The Wizard finished counting and began
to read his book:
The Princess turned into a bird in the sky.
She hid in a cloud, then she had one more try.

That was the end of the page. The Wizard
turned over to read more. But there was
no more. The next page in his book was
blank and white. He flew into a RAGE!

"YOU STUPID BOOK!" he shouted, and
he hurled it into the moat. The book landed
with a splash and sank to the bottom.
All the Wizard's magic was gone!

25

At that moment in the palace, the King and Queen and all the party guests came back to life.
"Where is Princess Eliza?" they asked each other.

Nobody knew except the Fairy Godmother,
and she only smiled and said nothing.

Princess Eliza had turned
herself from a white page
into a blue fish and was
swimming to the edge
of the moat.

She turned herself
into a yellow chick
and ran across the
corn in the farmyard.

She turned herself into
a green grasshopper
and hopped over
the grass.

She turned herself into an orange fox and raced through the orange leaves.

She turned herself into a purple butterfly and fluttered over the purple flowers.

She turned herself into a black cat and streaked through the black tunnel.

Then she turned herself into a white bird and flew . . .

. . . all the way back to the palace and in
through the window. She perched on a chair
at the tea table and changed herself . . .

back into a princess!

The King and Queen and all the party guests
hugged her. Then Princess Eliza cut her birthday
cake and everyone had a slice.